QUICKREADS

STUDENT BODIES

JANET LORIMER

SADDLEBACK
EDUCATIONAL PUBLISHING

QUICKREADS

SADDLEBACK
EDUCATIONAL PUBLISHING
www.sdlback.com

ISBN-13: 978-1-61651-219-4
ISBN-10: 1-61651-219-9
eBook: 978-1-60291-941-9

Printed in Guangzhou, China
0310/03-20-10

15 14 13 12 11   1 2 3 4 5

■ ■ ■

Jake Maguire emptied the dustpan into the trash can. Then he glanced around the big room.

From 8:00 to 5:00 the community college lounge was packed with day students, talking and laughing. But this time of night there were only a few students sitting at the tables. Most of them were quite a bit older and more serious than the daytime crowd.

Jake was glad there was less mess to clean up in the evenings. But he missed the lively presence of kids his own age.

"Hey, Maguire, get back to work!"

Jake jumped a foot. Old Ted Flannery—the head janitor—had a bad habit of sneaking up behind his assistants and scaring them. As if his weird black clothes and greasy black hair weren't scary enough!

Jake turned and glared at the old man. "I'm on it, okay?"

Ted chuckled. "Start cleaning those tables now. You know the drill: First wash them, and then wax them. I want this place spotless for tomorrow."

"Yeah, yeah," Jake muttered. He took the broom and dustpan to the janitor's closet.

While he filled a pail with water, Jake thought about how suddenly his life had changed for the worse.

■ ■ ■

Until a few weeks ago, Jake had thought his life was going great. He had a good job—the same one he'd held all through high school. His boss was all for kids going to college. He was glad to let Jake arrange his work schedule around his classes.

The day he registered for college, Jake had been lucky. He got all the classes he needed and he met Yolanda Melendez. To Jake, Yolanda seemed to be as perfect as any girl could be. She had a great sense of humor and the prettiest smile he'd ever seen. Best of all, she shared many of Jake's interests.

As luck would have it, they found they'd enrolled in the same French course. It was his only night class. He and Yolanda had agreed to study their French lessons together.

Then, just a couple of weeks later, Jake's whole world fell apart. First, his boss went out of business. That meant Jake needed another job right away. He'd been relieved to find the janitor's job on campus. But he'd had to drop out of the French class.

Jake was disappointed. But at least Yolanda had promised to study in the student lounge, so they could talk on his breaks.

So where was she? For the last couple of nights, there'd been no sign of her! Jake had called her cell phone several times but gotten no answer. Was she sick? Or maybe studying for a test? Or worse, had she met some other guy she liked better? Jake sure hoped she'd show up tonight. He was getting worried.

■ ■ ■

Jake tried to get his mind off Yolanda. He had to get those tables cleaned so he could go home.

He was polishing a table when the lights flickered. Jake glanced up. For some reason, he felt a chill. Was he imagining things, or had the temperature dropped? And why had the room suddenly become so quiet?

Glancing over his shoulder, Jake noticed a group of strange-looking people coming in. Several guys and a couple of girls stood in the doorway, looking around the room. They seemed to be searching for something—or someone.

Again, Jake felt a sudden chill. There was something very odd about this group—but he couldn't put his finger on it. Maybe it was that they were all dressed in black. Or maybe it was that they carried no books or backpacks. No—it was the strange look in their eyes. How could he explain it? It was a *hungry* look.

Get a grip, man! Back to work, Jake told himself. But he watched as they grabbed a table in the shadows at the back of the room. Sitting there, they stared at the other students intently. Jake could actually feel their cold, intense gaze. He hoped those creeps would be gone by the time he got to their table.

All of a sudden a big crowd of students poured into the lounge. Jake glanced at the clock. The last class had just ended. In a half-hour, the snack bar would close.

Jake spotted Ted frowning at him. If he didn't hurry, the old man would have his hide. He started to polish tables as fast as he could.

He was just finishing up when Ted flicked the lights off and on several times. That was the signal that the lounge was closing for the night.

■ ■ ■

Once outside, Jake headed for the parking lot. He was about halfway there when he saw a girl he knew from his history class. She was trying to attach a flyer to one of the bulletin boards, but her stapler kept jamming. Jake was about to go to her rescue when he saw someone dressed in black step out of the shadows.

"Hello, Carol," Jake heard the guy say. His voice was low and rough.

Carol turned toward him. "Uh—hello. Do I know you?" she asked.

"No, but you will," the guy said with a smile. Jake noticed how sharp his teeth looked in the moonlight.

He decided to step in. "Hey, there, Carol!" he yelled as he sprinted toward the nervous-looking girl.

Carol turned to see who had called out her name. As Jake got closer, the guy in black quickly pulled back into the shadows.

"Need any help?" Jake asked.

Carol grinned. "You're my hero!" she said. "I'm having a hard time getting these flyers up. The stapler keeps jamming." She handed it to him. "What happened to that other guy?" she asked, glancing around.

"Uh—I guess he left," Jake said.

Carol shrugged. "He was a strange one! I can't say I'm sorry he's gone."

Jake nodded. He glanced at the flyer as he stapled it to the bulletin board. The word MISSING was spelled out in big black letters across the top. Below was the photograph of a handsome young man.

"Who's this?" Jake asked.

"My—my brother," Carol said in a shaky voice. "He disappeared about a week ago," she went on. "I'm hoping someone will recognize his picture and get in touch with me."

"I'm sorry," Jake said. "I sure hope he turns up soon." Wanting to cheer her up, he added, "Probably he just took off on a road trip or something."

Carol shook her head. "We thought of that. But we've talked to all his friends—to everyone he knows, in fact. No one's seen a sign of him."

Jake frowned. "And your brother was a student here?"

Carol nodded. "You know, it's kind of weird. It seems that several students have gone missing recently."

Jake gazed at her in disbelief. "Really?" he said.

She pointed to other flyers on the bulletin board. Now Jake took a good look at them.

MISSING!
DISAPPEARED!
VANISHED!
Have you seen . . .?

He took a deep breath. And then it dawned on him. Where was Yolanda?

■ ■ ■

Jake walked Carol to her car in the parking lot.

"I used to feel safe walking around here at night. But now . . . Don't you think the campus seems kind of spooky this semester?" she asked.

"I don't know. This is my first semester here," Jake said.

"Take my word for it," Carol said. "Things changed when the semester started. We got a lot of new students like that guy back there—the one who stepped out of the shadows. I had a feeling that he didn't really have my best interests at heart."

"None of those kids in black are here during the day," Jake said. "Only at night. They give me the creeps, too."

Carol stopped at the next bulletin board to put up another flyer. "And those students aren't the only new people on campus," she said. "There are several new instructors and counselors, too. Some of them I like. The others . . ." She made a face.

Jake helped her with the flyer. "I guess I can't complain too much," he said. "One of the new counselors, Mr. Collins, put me onto my job. I'm not crazy about working nights. But if he hadn't helped me, I probably would have had to drop out."

Carol looked at Jake in surprise. "There are lots of day jobs on campus, Jake," she said. "Didn't Mr. Collins tell you about them?"

Jake was surprised. "Mr. Collins made it sound like that janitor's job was the only one left."

Carol shook her head. "There's something wrong with that," she said. "Maybe, for some reason, he didn't want you to work days."

They had reached Carol's car. Jake waited while she climbed in and locked the doors. Then she rolled the window down a crack.

Her face looked very serious. "Listen, Jake, be careful," she said. "I don't know what's going on. But you should know that every one of the kids who have disappeared were night school students."

■ ■ ■

When Jake got home, he noticed the light blinking on his answering machine. He pushed the play button and listened. The voice was familiar. It was Luis, Yolanda's brother. "Hey, Jake, we're trying to find Yolanda. Do you know where she is? Call me!"

Jake's stomach knotted up. He grabbed the phone and called Luis.

As late as it was, Luis answered on the second ring. "Yoli?" Luis yelled.

Jake could hear the panic in Luis' voice. "No, man, it's me, Jake. I just got your message. What's going on?"

"Thank God you called back, Jake. Do you have any idea where Yoli is?" Luis asked. "She hasn't been home for a couple of days. My folks are worried sick."

Jake felt sick, too. "I saw her two days ago. After French class she stopped by the student lounge. We only got to talk for about five minutes before old man Flannery jumped all over me. I told Yoli to wait until I was done so I could walk her to her car. But she was in a hurry to get home. I haven't seen her since."

Luis groaned. "My dad went to the cops, but they seem to think she's just another teenage runaway."

Jake exploded. "That's not true! I know how much Yolanda loves her family. She'd *never* just take off."

"I know," Luis agreed. "But the cops don't know her. And I don't think they care."

Then Jake told Luis about all the other students who had disappeared. "Something bad is going on," he said.

Luis was startled. "Can you talk to her teachers?" he asked. "Maybe one of them has seen her."

"No problem," Jake said. "I'll check it out. And I'll call tomorrow to let you know what I find out."

■ ■ ■

The next day Jake managed to talk to almost all of Yoli's teachers. They were all puzzled and concerned about Yolanda's disappearance. The only teacher he hadn't gotten to was Madame Broussard, the French teacher.

Jake decided to spend the afternoon studying in the library. But he was too distracted with worry to get much real studying done. *Where could she be?* he kept wondering. The sun was going down when he finally shoved his books into his backpack. He wanted to put his backpack in his car before he grabbed a bite to eat.

On his way back from the parking lot, Jake decided to take a shortcut. The dirt path was narrow and not well-lit, but it would save him some time.

The path ran beside a big old boarded-up building that was scheduled to be torn down soon. As Jake passed by, he had an eerie feeling that he was being watched. He glanced over at the boarded-up windows. Although he didn't see anyone, he couldn't shake the feeling that someone's eyes were following him. It made the hair on the back of his neck stand up. Jake walked faster.

Just ahead, the path veered into a small grove of trees. Jake hesitated and sucked in his breath. The shadows in the grove were thick and dark. Every nerve in his body seemed to scream, "Don't go in there!"

The snap of a twig made him jump. But there was no one else on the path! Now Jake was really getting scared.

"Hey, Jake!"

At the sound of his name, Jake spun around. Luis came stumbling out of the grove of trees!

"Man, am I glad to see you!" Luis cried out. "This part of the campus is really creepy at night."

Not nearly as glad as I am to see you, Jake thought. Instead he said, "What's up? Have you found Yolanda?"

Luis shook his head. "I talked to her

French teacher a while ago. She said she saw Yoli on campus last night. I still don't know what's going on—but at least I know that Yoli was around here yesterday. We've put up flyers all over campus. I have a good feeling we'll find her soon."

■ ■ ■

Jake gulped down a burger and fries at the snack bar. Then he went to the janitor's closet to get his broom and dustpan.

Now that he knew Yoli had been seen yesterday, he'd calmed down some. But where was she *now*? And why hadn't she gone home?

He felt a sudden flash of anger. *She'd better have a good answer,* he thought to himself.

It was almost time for the lounge to close when Yoli walked in! She was with the group of creepy students who'd come in the night before. Jake couldn't believe his eyes.

"Yoli!" he called out.

She stared right at him with no expression

on her face—no smile, nothing! Then she looked away.

Jake was stunned. What was going on? Why would a perfectly normal girl like Yolanda suddenly want to hang out with a bunch of freaks?

He stared as the group headed for the same table in the shadowy corner. It was then he realized how *different* Yolanda looked. She was wearing black jeans, a black shirt, and black boots. A black silk scarf was wound around her neck. Jake had never seen her dress like that. She was a girl who loved to wear bright colors.

Jake had had enough. Suddenly he didn't care what old man Flannery thought. He put down his broom and stormed over to Yoli's table.

"Where have you been, Yoli?" he demanded. "Your family is almost sick with worry. Luis has been running around everywhere looking for you."

Yoli said nothing. She just stared at him as if she'd never seen him before. Then she turned away.

Jake was angry and hurt. But then Yoli turned away and the scarf around her neck slipped down. There were two small red marks on the side of her throat! Jake gasped in horror.

One of the guys at the table stood up. He stepped in front of Yolanda as if to protect her. Jake could have sworn that his eyes were glowing red!

But when Jake blinked and looked again, the glow was gone. Now the stony-faced guy looked like he was ready to tear Jake's heart out.

"Leave her alone," the freaky guy said in a threatening voice.

Jake was furious. "You think you can stop me?" he snarled.

Then the freak grinned. "Or maybe you'd like to join us, Jake? Do you want to be with Yolanda forever?"

The guy's strange words and ugly smile hit Jake like a bucket of ice water. In shock, he just stood there staring. The freak and his friends laughed at him—until they suddenly spotted something behind Jake.

He turned to see what had caught their attention. It was only Madame Broussard, the French teacher, and Jake's counselor, Mr. Collins. The two of them were standing by the snack bar, talking.

All moving as one, the strange students stood and started walking toward the door. Yolanda's fingers brushed against Jake's hand as she passed by. Her skin was as cold as ice!

The moment the students left, Jake pulled out his cell phone to call Luis.

As usual, Ted Flannery appeared out of nowhere. "Put that phone away, Maguire! What's the matter with you? You've got a lot of work to do," the old man growled.

Jake stared at Ted. "I'm sorry, but this is an emergency," Jake snapped. "Yolanda's brother—"

"Yeah, I know," Ted said. "Luis was in here earlier, showing her picture around. Listen, kid, take it from me—you really don't want to get involved in this situation."

Jake ignored his boss and made his call. But all he got was Luis' voice- mail. Then, shoving the cell phone back in his pocket, he started for the door. Ted Flannery ran up to him and grabbed his arm. "Maguire! Where do you think you're going?"

Jake pulled his arm away. "If you want to fire me, fire me," he said in a tired voice. "But you can't stop me! Yolanda needs my help!"

■ ■ ■

Outside, Jake spotted Yolanda and her weird friends heading across campus. He followed closely behind as they approached the old boarded up building. Hidden in shadow, Jake watched as they slipped under a loose board and disappeared inside.

He leaned against a nearby tree and considered his options. Call the police? Keep trying to get in touch with Luis? Contact campus security?

A little voice in the back of his mind told him to connect the dots. First, there was Yoli's

sudden disappearance . . . the black clothing
. . . her cold skin . . . the red marks on her
neck . . .

Vampires! The word was thrilling if you
were talking about a late-night horror show.
But it was terrifying if you actually had to
go up against the living dead!

Jake shook his head. He knew the cops
would laugh at his unlikely story. Or worse
yet, arrest him. Same with campus security.
As for Luis, Jake was pretty sure that
Yolanda's brother would think he'd lost his
mind.

"I've got to do this by myself," Jake
groaned. "But how?"

He thought about every vampire movie
he'd ever seen. He remembered that
vampires were afraid of garlic, but he
didn't think it would kill them. Then he
remembered a movie character killing a
vampire by driving a wooden stake through
its heart!

But this wasn't the movies, and Jake was
badly outnumbered. And not only that, but

the very thought of driving a stake into living flesh was unimaginable.

The worst of it was trying to figure out what to do about Yolanda. Jake felt a lump form at the back of his throat.

"Oh, Yoli," he whispered sadly. There was no way he could hurt Yoli—let alone drive a stake through her heart. Then he noticed that the lights were still on in the library. That gave him an idea.

"I'll hang out there until closing," Jake decided. "I can get on one of the library computers and go online. Maybe I can do a search and come up with some way to save her."

Luckily, he was able to get online almost at once. It was amazing how many websites he found that dealt with the undead. Some of the sites were meant to be "horror show" funny, but others were very serious.

In the next couple of hours, Jake learned more about vampires than he'd ever thought possible. He also found several ways to kill them.

But first there was something important he had to figure out. Who was the head vampire? Who had come on campus recently to establish this new nest of undead creatures?

Then he remembered how intensely the students in black had gazed at Mr. Collins and Madame Broussard. And he thought about something Carol had said: *All the trouble had started at the beginning of the semester*—the same time the new teachers and counselors had arrived.

Something else occurred to him, too. Ted Flannery seemed to know what was going on. Why else would he have warned Jake to stay out of it? So who was the chief bloodsucker?

He glanced at his watch and decided to lay low for a few more hours. But before he went into hiding, he needed some things he could use to destroy the vampires. First, Jake headed for the student lounge and then drove to a nearby drugstore.

■ ■ ■

After collecting his weapons, Jake stowed them in his car and curled up in the back seat. He was exhausted. One minute he was planning how to get into the boarded-up building. It seemed just a minute later when he opened his eyes. Jake sat up fast and glanced at his watch. The sun was already coming up!

"Oh, no, I fell asleep!" he groaned. "It won't be long before the campus is crawling with people. I've got to get going if I want to save Yoli."

He grabbed his weapons and climbed out of the car. His hands were shaking, and he was breathing fast.

He took the shortcut path toward the old building. He knew that vampires needed shelter from the daylight. By now, they would all be back in their nest—and hopefully, asleep. If not—

Jake found the loose board and quietly slipped under it. The air inside was thick with the stench of rotting meat. He wrinkled his nose at the terrible smell and waited for his eyes to adjust to the darkness. Then he peered around. He was standing in what had been the lobby. It was empty. He tiptoed across the dusty floor toward the door into the main room.

Pausing in the doorway, he stared in disbelief. The floor was littered with the bodies of the missing students! He recognized Carol's brother and the faces of several other students whose pictures were on the bulletin boards.

Suddenly, the realization of what he was about to do hit him. *How can I kill all these people!* his mind cried out. *They didn't ask for this!*

Then he remembered something he'd read on the Internet. *These students can still be saved!* he thought. *By killing only the head vampire, I can release them from—*

"Are you looking for me? I'm back here, Jake. Right behind you."

Jake jumped and turned around. Just

a few feet away stood the creature he was looking for. Not a him—a her! Madame Broussard, the queen of the undead.

■ ■ ■

Jake gasped and quickly backed away, almost falling down.

When Madame Broussard smiled, he saw how white and sharp her teeth were! "I was so sad when you dropped my class," the French teacher said softly. She moved toward him the way a snake slithers toward its victim. "I'm glad you're here. Now you can become a member of our little family."

"I don't think so," Jake said as he struggled to focus his attention. He'd need to be in just the right spot to carry out his plan. Madame took another slow step forward, but Jake was already dashing toward the bodies on the floor. Madame Broussard laughed. "Oh, Jake! Do you think it's that easy to get away from me?"

Jake didn't bother to answer. He was desperately looking around for Yolanda.

Suddenly, he spotted her. She was curled up in a corner, looking as if she were taking a nap.

Jake reached down and shook her. "Yoli," he said. "Wake up!" Her eyelids fluttered, then shut again.

"She can't hear you, Jake," Madame Broussard said as she slithered toward him. "Give it up, Jake. It's time for you to become one of us."

Now she was just a couple of feet away. Jake's heart pounded with fear as she threw back her head and opened her mouth wide. Her sharp fangs gleamed in the dim light.

Now, thought Jake as he pulled a spray can from his jacket pocket. He aimed it at her face. When he pushed the button, a thick white liquid frosted her hair and skin. It covered her mouth and nose and dripped onto her clothes.

The French teacher gazed down at herself in surprise. "You can't be serious, Jake. What is this?" she scoffed. "Canned garlic? Ha! I don't think so."

"No, it's furniture wax," Jake said.

Madame's eyes opened wide. Then she burst out laughing. "Furniture wax? And what did you plan to do with that, Jake? *Polish* me to death?"

"Not quite," Jake growled as he pulled a lighter from his other pocket. Flicking the lever, he held the lighter in front of him. Then he positioned the spray can behind the flame, his finger poised on the button.

Madame Broussard suddenly realized Jake's plan. Now her eyes showed nothing but fear—but it was too late! As Jake's finger pressed the button, the flare from his makeshift flame thrower engulfed her. In a moment, Madame Broussard's body turned into a blazing torch.

"This stuff burns fast," Jake said—but his words were lost in her screams. She was flailing her arms trying to put out the flames. But her efforts were useless. She fell to the floor, and within moments all that was left of her was a pile of ash.

Now, all around him, Jake could hear

the groans of students slowly coming back to life. He rushed toward Yolanda, who was whimpering softly.

Jake knelt down and took Yolanda in his arms. "It's all right," he whispered. "You're safe now."

She blinked, like someone waking from a deep coma. "Where are we, Jake? Did I doze off? Is it time for class?" she asked in a groggy voice.

Jake grinned and hugged her. "There's no school today, Yoli," he said. "It's time for you—all of you—to go home!"

After-Reading Wrap-Up

1. Do you think *Student Bodies* is an interesting title for this story? Explain why or why not.

2. Could you identify with the main character, Jake Maguire? Under the same circumstances, would you have done what he did? In what ways might you have behaved differently?

3. Jake was motivated by his desire to find Yolanda. What motivated some of the other characters? Why did Mr. Collins, for example, want Jake to work nights?

4. In the story, Jake climbs under a loose board to enter an abandoned building. Have you ever explored an uninhabited old building? If so, describe what you saw there. If not, describe what you imagine you might find in such a place.

- Continued -

5. Reread the scenes that include Carol, Jake's friend from history class. Why do you think the author created this character?

6. What did you think when you learned the truth about the weird students dressed in black? Were you surprised? What clue about them did Jake pick up earlier when he spoke to Yoli in the cafeteria?